That Girl with the Red Hair:

A Jo Danning Short Story

Rae T. Alexander

To

The lovers of magic and mystery everywhere

1

2

3

4

5

6

7

8

9

1

Chapter 1

"How did you kill her?"—Jason wanted answers. He wanted to hear everything. He wanted it all. He could almost taste it.

"Are you here to break me?" the chained and drugged prisoner asked.

Jason walked around the table and faced him.

"I don't give a shit!" Jason said, as he sat down in front of him and took out his apple and knife.

"You don't mind if I eat, do you?" he asked, as he slowly peeled the red fruit. Jason let the juice flow over his fingers as he cut it. The liquid dripped down on the table, and his eyes quickly darted back at the prisoner.

"Is that how it felt?" Jason asked, as he chewed his first piece. "The blood on your fingers?" He savored the crunch and allowed the juice to leak from his lips, and he added with a lazy slur, "Sloppy and juicy?"

The man lunged forward suddenly, but his chains held him in the metal chair.

"She had a minor defect. You would not understand," he spit out. He was so drugged that he could not make out the features of his visitor. The ringing in his ears did not allow him to completely understand his tone or meaning. The inept guards had overdosed him to keep him calm.

"Then—make me understand. Make me understand, Shawn," Jason said, as he took another bite.

Jason wasn't even a cop. Jason was no detective. He wasn't with the government.

He thought of himself as a consultant. He was there on an "as needed" basis. He was self-employed.

Jason was concerned that Shawn would not talk, but he did.

"She was scared," Shawn said. "I smelled her fear from the parking lot—long before I killed her. She fumbled around for her keys, just before she opened her front door. I followed her real slow— just so I could watch her. Her fear was so intoxicating." He licked his lips.

Jason continued eating his apple while the killer poured out his soul to him.

"I broke in," Shawn said. "I waited until I thought she was almost asleep. I wanted to see her face when I broke into her apartment.

"I waited for two hours. I sat at her bedside and stared at her beautiful white face. I held my knife in my hands, anxious for the moment. I wanted to see her suffer. That is why I killed her. I wanted to see her suffer. I like to see people suffer."

Jason finished his apple and left the apple core and the peeling on the table. He reached into his brown jacket for a napkin taken from a restaurant earlier that morning. He got up from his chair and wiped his mouth and hands. He pulled out a handcuff key from his right jean pocket and placed it on top of the apple core. He balanced it slowly and carefully while he checked the expression on the prisoner. The action made the young man stop his tale. He gave Jason a curious look of confusion, but he still could not see him clearly.

Shawn watched the blurry figure, as he saw the most curious act of all. Jason walked behind the table slowly. He stepped up to the prisoner and reached behind his back. He used a generic key and removed the lock from the chains. He left the handcuffs on Shawn, but he pulled his chains away from him.

Jason stepped away while his eyes stayed on Shawn. He walked to the door of the interrogation room, but Shawn called him back.

"Wait!" he said to Jason with concern and a half-frowning puzzlement. "You ain't the doctor?" Shawn glanced back at the handcuff key on the apple core. Evidence of insanity was the prisoner's goal, but the wrong audience viewed the act.

"No," Jason told him, as he turned around at the door. He walked back to the table with limited information. "Shawn, you really bore the hell out of me."

"Who are you?" Shawn asked. He prepared himself for another lunge, but he stayed on his chair.

"Maybe I'll tell you later—maybe not," Jason said. "I like to see people suffer also—especially scumbags like you." Shawn bent his mouth into a frown, and then he looked back at the key.

Jason left the room and walked down the hallway where he passed a guard. The guard assumed by looking at Jason's street clothes that he was a detective—so Jason played along.

"Careful with that prisoner. He is wild tonight," Jason told him—as he turned another corner and headed for the kitchen exit.

A minimal-security room in the basement served as a jail for the prisoner. Jason exited through a door at the end of a long hallway. It was an exit least likely to draw attention—there was no alarm on the door. There was barely a doorknob. The screws were loose. The jail needed many improvements, but the county was low on funds. Jason wished that he could have stayed to see the prisoner's expression when the real detective came to question him—but he did what was needed. He set the trap.

Jason walked to his silver Corvette and opened the door. Just before he got inside, he stepped to the rear of the car and threw up the apple pieces. He knelt in the white sun-drenched sand beside his car. Drips of blood dangled around his mouth as he heaved a white and red liquid.

His body bowed in a shape of a forceful worship. Drops of sweat gathered on his suntanned forehead and dripped to the ground. He felt his forehead for signs of a fever as he stood up. He wiped his mouth with a quick brush of his sleeve. His eyes were watery, as he got back into his car.

He rolled down his window, and looked at the sage and weeds in the dirt. A butterfly flew away after its breakfast, and Jason wished for his own freedom. In some ways, he envied the position of the prisoner.

The prisoner was contained, but the next move was up to him. Shawn at least had freedom. Jason, however, was compelled to do everything that he was doing. He had no freedom. He had a mission to accomplish. In addition to that, his body fought a cancer that was eating up his insides and growing stronger every day.

Inside the deficient cell, the killer made his decision and used the key. He killed one person and injured another to get outside of the compound. A maximum-security area, twenty miles away, was to be the next holding area for Shawn. However, during the changing of the guard, a careless guard lost his focus for only five seconds, and that was enough.

This Mohave town was too small to handle the situation, even for just an overnight stay. The jail failed to hold Shawn, but Jason already predicted that. Jason was waiting for him. If there had been another way, Jason would have taken it. The recent deaths of three women and two children pushed him forward. Shawn was a suspected serial killer in several small towns in the South, primarily in North Carolina and Georgia. Women were his favorite toys, but Shawn's playtime was almost over.

Jason turned the ignition, and then he got out of the car to pick a few of the weeds out of the dirt, near the butterfly's food. He stuffed a few of them in his pocket, and then he turned and saw him. He watched the small county jail as Shawn suddenly came rushing out of a grey door.

Jason got back in and revved the engine. He slammed the car door as he moved forward. Dirt shot away from the rear tires as he bolted away from the flying dirt and crossed the black broken pavement of the main highway. He crashed through the chain-linked fence and aligned his weapon.

The Corvette hit Shawn and threw him to the right side of the vehicle. For good measure, Jason stopped the car and backed over the body, and then he ran over him once more going forward.

He looked in his mirror as he sped out of the fenced area and back to the highway. Smoke from the burning tires said their farewell to the little dusty town.

2

Chapter 2

Jo walked to the tiny office with a cramp in her stomach. She wasn't used to working. Small things like jobs scared her. It had been a few months since her last job—the military. Being a security specialist and being a newspaper columnist were two very different things.

"Jo! Sit down," the impatient and overweight man directed.

The man pushed aside his sausage and cheese biscuit and wiped his mouth with a thin paper napkin. Several leftover crumbs remained in his moustache.

Jo obeyed and slowly took a seat in the squeaky chair, in front of his unvarnished desk. It was her second meeting with him, but she was still startled by the bold voice of Harry Fisher.

"Josey had the job before you, you know," Harry said. "And I only agreed to take you on for a week or two—on a trial basis. But I'll be damned if I put up with more people coming in here and nosing around my business. This is entirely your fault!"

"Mr. Fisher, I apologize for those men coming in and asking all those questions. It won't happen again. I can assure you of that," Ms. Danning told him.

A few days before, Jo Danning had casually agreed that she would consider working for a government agency as a consultant. She told Mr. Jackson that she would "think about it," but the agency had only heard the word, "Yes." They performed a little background investigation on her, including her friends, relatives, and job prospects.

"I thought that you were through with the military and all that shit!" Harry said.

"I am," Jo told him. "And I really need this job, if nothing but for my sanity's sake. Please don't fire me."

Harry was an outspoken man, but he was just a loudmouth for the most part. He smiled back at her and tossed a file to the front of his desk, in front of Jo's concerned and curious eyes.

"What's this?" she asked.

"Some of Josey's files. You can start with this. Her office is the third door on the left, down the hallway," Harry said. "You type up some responses. Show 'em to my editor...and we shall see."

"And, Jo?" he added, as Jo got up from her chair, picked up the file, and smiled. "No controversial stuff."

At a recommendation of a friend, Harry had given Jo her first interview a few days before. She was to replace Josey Castor, the advice columnist and local gossip for the Wilmington paper.

"How is your son doing?" Harry asked her, as she got to the office door. He did not care. He was just wrapping up.

"My little botanist is doing just fine. Thank you, Mr. Fisher," Jo said.

"Good," Harry said with a stuffed mouth, as he motioned her out of his office. He had a newspaper to run.

Jo took her precious new files, full of letters from Josey's readers, and walked out. She beamed with renewed confidence as she walked to her new office. She could barely contain her relief while her uncomfortable interview shoes clicked the concrete floor with a pace that was almost like a skip.

When she opened her door, she was surprised to see a young lady looking through the drawers of her desk.

"Oh, sorry," Jo said. "Maybe this is the wrong room."

The teenager stopped what she was doing and looked up at Jo.

"Nah, this is it," she told Jo. "This was Josey's office. I was just getting out some personal crap of hers. My name is Judy." She offered a smile, but she refused a hand to Jo.

"Oh, you're the temp," Jo said, as Judy gave her a frown. That word disparaged her.

"I am supposed to be your secretary, sort of—I think," Judy told her. "I am at the end of the hallway." She smacked her gum as she explored the desk.

Judy told her that she was the new secretary to several of the writers on the staff. The newspaper hired minimal-wage workers in college to move papers from the writers to the editorial staff, make appointments, write stories, fetch coffee, and learn the "business." She was a gopher. She was also a woman that usually wore her red hair long. That day, however, it was tied up and held back with rubber bands and pins.

Jo found out some juicy gossip from Judy. Josey had passed away from a heart attack while doing her usual exercises at a local gym and visiting her gay "friend." She had loads of friends, and she had even more followers—men, women, and even children.

"What's that?" Jo asked Judy. She pointed at a picture in Judy's hand. The last item in the back of the left desk drawer was a photo of Josey on a torn magazine cover.

"It kinda looks like Josey. I saw her picture before," Judy said. "I'm new."

Judy left the office, but she gave the magazine cover to an insistent Jo. She wanted to size up her predecessor. Does everyone that works here have red hair, she thought.

"Meh," Jo said, as she looked at the red curls in the photo. It wasn't Josey's best photo, but it was average. Jo pumped up her blonde hair and pouted her red lips.

She sat down in her padded chair and opened the thick file from Harry. She wanted to see what was in the letters to Josey. She was ready for her first intrusion into the personal lives of avid readers, but she was interrupted by a knock against the side of the open door of her office.

Jo looked up, not expecting guests, and saw a girl with black hair and brown skin. She had twirly black hair that fell indiscriminately on her forehead and ears. She looked about ten, or maybe older. Jo wasn't sure. Her son was thirteen, but he was a boy. Her age was difficult to judge.

"Can I help you?" Jo said with an inviting expression.

The girl walked to a chair in front of Jo's desk and sat down. She had a dress that was muddy in appearance, and Jo noticed that she was barefooted.

"I need you to write about something," she told her. "I didn't want to ask you in a letter."

Jo looked down at her phone on her desk. She had the sudden urge to call Judy and ask her to explain how visitors were able to simply walk into the place without being properly screened. After her experience, in Taylor, North Carolina, she was apprehensive about entertaining strangers. After all, she had seen a ghost before. She didn't want that episode to repeat. This girl seemed odd.

"My mom is going to have a baby soon," she said. "Some of my family wants my mama to have an abortion."

That was a surprise, Jo thought. This new job was going to be fascinating, but she was under strict orders—nothing controversial. Jo wanted to keep her job. She watched the girl scratch her face that was speckled with spots of black and brown dirt. Jo did not know how to respond. She felt the need to name the stranger.

"I am sorry, um," Jo said, as she leaned on her elbows.

"Brea," she said. "My name is Brea."

"I am sorry, Brea," Jo apologized. "I don't, or rather…"

The girl got up and stormed to the door in anger, but she turned back.

"I knew you wouldn't help me!" she yelled.

She bumped into a man in a dirty brown leather jacket as she left the room. He looked back at her as she ran down the hall and away from Jo's office. That caught Jo's attention.

"You can *see* her?" Jo asked him, as she got up and walked to the doorway.

"Yes. Why?" he asked.

"Nothing," Jo said. She was calm because she knew that her premature fears of a ghost sighting were over. She was just a little girl, Jo thought.

Jo went back to her desk and plopped down on the wooden seat. She clutched the sides of her face with trembling hands, when she suddenly remembered the visitor was watching her with some concern.

"Are you ok?" he asked.

"Sorry," Jo smiled. "Need more coffee. What can I do for you?"

The morning was busy, she thought, even without the letters.

Is this how it is going to be?

The man pushed back brown hair and sat down.

"I need your help," he said. "I am a crime-scene consultant. I need your help to track down a serial killer. My name is Jason." He reached a rugged hand out to her.

"Jason Webb"

3

Chapter 3

The entrance to the building was not secure. There were no security guards. The lobby was easily accessible to the curious. Plants greeted Jo as she walked toward the elevator. They were not real, but it was a nice touch. Miniature trees decorated the walkway and stood in plastic planters on the black and polished floor.

She rode the elevator to the top and exited on the third floor. Her destination was the office of the Millford and King Seed Company of North Carolina. Mr. Jackson greeted her when she opened the door that simply read, "M&K Office."

"Ms. Danning," he said. "Welcome. Have you decided yet?

"Mr. Jackson," she began, as he escorted her to an office in the rear.

"Ken," Mr. Jackson said and corrected while he walked. "I think we can jump to first names, right?"

The front waiting room that they passed on the way to his office seemed surprisingly artificial. This was her first visit. She found the address on the internet, from a business card that Ken had given to her on a beach, the day that he had first met her.

Ken sat down, but Jo stood in defiance.

"How dare you come down to my office and spy on me!" Jo said.

Mr. Jackson explained that it was necessary for the government clearance, in case she agreed to be part of "the team."

"I am not surprised, you know?" Ken said. "They always come around—although, the gift doesn't always last." Ken saw both the anger and doubt in her frown.

"Still don't believe?" he asked her. She looked away and

scanned his stoic room of carefully placed books with generic titles on bookshelves that were rectangular—and too perfect. The only thing that stood out to Jo was the plain brown wall to Ken's right. There were photos of weeds and plants, and even a generic company logo—but nothing else.

Ken saw the look on Jo's face that said, "Tell me more." He got up with a smirk, walked to the photo of the company logo, and pressed a button, hidden in the polished dark wood. A door in the wall formed, and then it retreated and moved to the side. Before Ken could gesture her inside, Jo was already on her way.

She walked ahead of him and into the room of computers, maps, stacked photos, and files of crime data. This looked more appropriate for a secret government headquarters, she thought.

Ken explained that it was only the Wilmington division and pointed out the scenery to her.

"My tech is on lunch," Ken said. "But here are the crime data cases that we are looking at today." He picked up a random file and handed it to her. "Don't worry. We cleared you, remember?"

"It won't happen again," Ken promised. He exchanged his wink and a smile for a more serious gaze. Jo thought it was too forward and turned away from his annoying look with the file in her hands.

"See that it doesn't," she said and sighed.

The secret government group was interested in Jo because of a gift that she was too frightened to believe in. Her only other experience in the government had been with linguistics, in the Air Force.

Her phone buzzed in her pocket as she glanced at some photos and tossed the folder down forcibly on a metal table nearby.

"Sick!" she said, as she answered the phone and walked to a

window composed of a one-way substance. Light came through, but no one could see inside from the streets. That was their security. She was glad to trade the view of the corpse in the folder for the boring sights of Elder Street, in Wilmington.

"Casey?" Jo asked. It was her son. He wanted to tell her about something that she had given him on the night before. It was a weed to everyone else, but to him it was a scientific discovery.

"But Mom," he interrupted.

Jo explained that she was in the middle of something and that he could share his science with her when she got home. "They let kids take cell phones to school?"—she mumbled it out loud.

"Not the school that *he* goes to," Agent Jackson said. Jo became angry again at the remark.

"What the hell?" Jo said. "You checked the *school* also?"

Jo started to walk away with an impulsive determination and uttered, "Screw this." She reached the opening in the wall that had just closed. As she looked for a button to open it, she suddenly realized why she had come to see Ken. She closed her eyes tightly and squinted away momentary tears, and then she turned and faced the agent. Ken felt it without the words.

"It happened again, didn't it?" he said. "Jo, you have got to trust me. I have seen it all."

He had not seen it all, but it sounded very impressive—to him.

"I thought that it did," Jo said. "But then someone jolted me back to reality. I came here because I was approached by someone looking into a murder case."

"Oh, is that all?" Ken said. He was relieved, but he was frustrated at the same time.

"I have serious cases that need your attention," he said to her. "I am not running a service for your gossip column fans. Take that one you just looked at, for example. Did you sense anything? Anything at all?"

"Look," she said as she walked to him. "First of all, I only had the experience one time. Maybe I was just seeing things. Maybe it was a trick. And even if I did believe it, I don't know how it works. No—I didn't see anything or feel anything at all."

Jo asked Ken about the photo in the file. He told her that it was the photo of a victim. It was death at the hands of a killer that liked to kill little girls—always little girls with red hair. She then told Ken about her two visitors, in spite of his initial look and speech of disapproval.

"Sorry. It was my first day on the job, and I had a weird girl and a cop come into my office. I was freaked out, I suppose," she said and then changed the subject. "What happened to the girl in the photo?"

"That first photo in the file was of the little girl. Her name was Pamela. Beautiful girl," Ken said. "She was walking home from school and abducted. It must have taken at least a hundred scratches with the knife to kill her. He took his time. He liked it. A lot!

"We thought that we had a suspect. But then he came up with an alibi—an ironclad one. He was with a former Marine Officer. The guy's record was impeccable. The victim's mother was going to talk. I think that she knew what happened…but…"

"Dead?" Jo asked, as she went back to the window. Ken confirmed it.

"Strangled. And she had a broom that was shoved up her vagina. It was rammed through her intestinal walls. We found her with her legs spread open. Her nipples were cut off and placed on her eyelids." He paused and added, "Does this gross you out?…This is the kind of serious stuff that we have here, Jo."

Jo repeated again that she sensed or saw nothing that would help him. At that moment, she felt that the job was probably not for her. It was sickening, and she was not able to contribute. Perhaps, she thought, the so-called gift was a one-time experience.

Jo forgot that there were two odd experiences in Taylor. She had seen one ghost, but she had seen him twice. She was beginning to get it out of her system. It was time to enjoy her new life in Wilmington—free of ghosts and free of Mr. Jackson.

Kenneth shook her out of her thoughts as he continued.

"This guy—this alibi of his—I was suspicious. It was a little too neat. I was going to have him followed, but he disappeared. A witness said that he mentioned to someone in a bar that he was heading to somewhere in California—but there are no records of him being on any flight out of the state. He just disappeared. His car is missing, but he probably changed the plates on it. The suspect disappeared also. They had to be in on everything—together. The suspect used a fake ID and left without a trace. Dead ends…all I got."

Jo walked away from the window and back to the table where the file rested and opened it up. She gave a confident look to Ken. She was determined that a *man* was not going to be braver than she was. She swallowed heavily as she skipped the briefs and only viewed the photos.

Her body froze as she looked at the very last picture.

The agent was familiar with the look. She found something, he thought. His prior consultants used to have the same look—during their moment of discovery.

"What is it," Ken said and approached. He looked down at the photo. It was a picture of the killer's alibi.

18

"This was the man that came to visit me," she said, as she pointed a stiff finger at the print. "This is Jason Webb. This was Shawn's alibi." She closed the file that read, "Shawn Harris."

4

The rock music blasted through the thin walls and into the old street. The man inside the tiny apartment looked outside his unclean window and saw the bothersome intruders. It was a man and a woman. They did not belong in that neighborhood.

He got up and began to hide his paraphernalia that had helped him with his anxiety on the night before. He suspected it was going to be a drug bust. The sounds of the knocks on his door frightened him, almost into a full and false confession. The raps continued, as he dragged his bare feet across the dirty floor littered with rat poop and dried food.

He opened and peeked out the door, but he kept the chain on.

"Yeah?" he said to Jo and Ken.

They wanted to know where Janine was. She was the sister and former roommate of the murdered woman. Ken insisted that they were not there to turn him in. They needed information only. Once Jo learned that the victim had a sister, she insisted on talking to her. She was curious about Jason Webb and his whole connection to this, and she did not like the idea of a strange man following her around. What if he went after Casey, she thought. She had called the school just to be sure that Casey was safe, just before they arrived at this wrong side of town. The wrong side of town was the kind of place where weird things happened—at least, for Jo.

Ken busted the door open, after the man refused to answer any questions and stepped away. The chain hit the wall with a snap, and Agent Jackson drew his gun. Jo rolled her eyes at the unnecessary and unimpressive action. She went into the bedroom and found the man crouched at the end of his bed with his chin on his knees. She remembered a friend in the Air Force who was a "druggy." She wasn't scared at all. Ken holstered his embarrassment and his gun.

Johnny "Cracker" was his name. He told them that Janine had come into some money. She lived in an apartment on Howe Avenue and Third Street.

"She's getting married," Johnny said. "That's all I know. She's moving away, and I took over her last month of rent—actually I owe for two weeks, dude."

"Your place smells like shit, Johnny," the agent said, as he swaggered in front of Jo.

Blood dripped out of Johnny's nose, and he smeared it on his cheek with a quick wipe. He saw a speck of red on his hand through blurry vision and panicked. Johnny wiped his hands on each arm and ran to a bathroom sink, while Jo held back Ken from going after him.

Jo slowly followed Johnny into the bathroom and eyed him in his pajamas and standing over the dirty sink. He kept washing his hands under a small dribble of water and grabbing a filthy towel to clean them. He had to get rid of the blood. Ken soon came up behind her with his own suspicions.

"Where is that blood from?" Ken bellowed.

"He has a damn bloody nose, you idiot," Jo said and closed the bathroom door on him.

She took over and attended Johnny like a nurse or an angel. She recalled the day that she lost a friend in Germany. She remembered the visions and the dreams and the final insanity of her friend Kathy. She helped Johnny clean up and instructed him to keep his head back, then she opened the door. Ken was exploring the musty bedroom. He stopped, as Jo assisted Johnny back to his bed.

On the floor were nude photos, ripped out of a magazine, and there was a jar of lubricant beside the bed. It was a jar of petroleum, and there was a kitchen knife stuck inside. Ken's imagination began again.

"Johnny, where did the knife come from?" Ken asked him. A trembling Johnny began to cry, and he turned his bloody nose down into a discolored pillow. He grabbed the yellow-stained sheets, wrapped them over his body, and hid underneath the smelly fabric.

"I don't know anything, man," Johnny cried out.

"Can we leave now?" Jo asked the agent. She was tired of inflicting so much pain on the suffering young man.

"You may be right," the agent said and gave up. He turned away from the bed and escorted Jo out of the bedroom. "You ain't cut out for this."

As they walked to the front door, a cat jumped out toward them, from behind the refrigerator, to the left of the front door. Ken stumbled against the wall to balance his fall, but it was too late. He slipped and fell on the floor.

"Gross," Ken said, as he landed on a gooey brown liquid.

Jo laughed as she helped him up, and she almost slipped on some grease and fell down on top of him. For a brief moment, they both laughed like old friends. A voice from the bedroom asked them if they were ok. Johnny almost seemed human to the agent.

Ken slipped one more time at the door, and his hand slid back behind the refrigerator. His sleeve caught a metal clip on the back of the appliance. It tore his jacket, but it stabilized him.

"Maybe *I* need a nurse *also*," he mocked, but Jo was not taken in by his flirtatious gab. The laughter was gone. She stepped out of the apartment and into the hallway. She marched to the end of the corridor, out of the small and run-down complex, and waited for him near his car. Let him clean up his own mess, she thought.

Ken wiped the grease off with some newspaper on the floor. He walked out of the building, as he straightened his clothes and his hair. He was not showing off his best stuff to the lady. He got into the car and looked in his mirror for any more signs of shame, while Jo got into the vehicle with a question.

"You didn't touch Johnny, did you," a puzzled Jo said, as she interrupted his beauty treatment. She buckled her seatbelt and closed the car door.

"No—why?" he asked.

Jo pointed to her middle finger, but Ken did not get it. With a sigh, she pointed to his finger, while she had to stretch her seatbelt to reach his left hand. It was a speck of blood.

They rushed back inside the apartment. The door was still unlocked, and Johnny was still under the covers in his bedroom.

Ken took out a small flashlight from his shirt pocket. He shined it behind the refrigerator and saw nothing but dust, cobwebs, and mounds of cat hair. Jo opened the appliance while he explored behind it.

"Agent Jackson," she said, as she backed away and slammed the door. "I'm going to be sick," Jo said, as she rushed to the bathroom. Ken soon heard the sounds of her vomit hitting the toilet water, just as he opened the refrigerator that was full of dissected surprises.

There were dozens of clear plastic bags that were unevenly sealed with duct tape. It was a sloppy job, but it was sufficient. Several bags had pieces of arms, while others had the parts of a leg. Juice pooled in the bottom of the bags, as it oozed out of the body parts. On the top shelve were bags of organs, ears, and a nose.

24

Ken opened the freezer, after he shut the bottom door. That action solved part of his case. The eyes had been removed, and empty sockets looked back at him, as if they were trying to say something. It was the decapitated head of Jason Webb.

5

Ken Jackson paced around in the crime lab, while his assistant, Annette, reviewed the blood results. Ken told Jo that Annette was the only other person that knew about her gifts. *She* was also classified.

Annette pushed away her bright auburn hair while she ate a greasy cheese sandwich, purchased from the local burger joint. Her mouth was full when she made the announcement.

"A definite match. Even the dental records confirmed it," she said as she munched. She handed the folder to Ken, and he attempted to wipe the grease stains off the papers. He was annoyed, but she was valuable. Jo thought that she was useless and unnecessary. Of course, it was Jason, Jo thought. Didn't the head say it all?

How many red heads are there in this town, Jo thought.

Annette once had the "gift." She had the ability to look at other realms and talk to dead people. However, as Ken had frequently told Jo, gifts were not always permanent or predictable. Many consultants lost their capabilities and insight and resigned, but a few of those people stayed behind and continued to work with the secret group of men that had no name and hid behind a fictitious seed company.

"Mama!" the child cried out. It was the voice of Annette's little girl, outside, at the corner ice-cream parlor. The school bus driver and the principle agreed to drop her off at the shop every day, just across where "mama" worked. It was a convenient arrangement and a perfect excuse to leave work early—a nightmare for a boss, but Annette was worth it. Ken once had a "thing" for her.

Jo detected the attraction between Annette and the agent. He was a goofball, and quite annoying. Perhaps, this is the only kind of person that could work this job, she thought. He reminded her of a television detective. He was too suave and too literal most of the time. He often overkilled his remarks and called attention to himself. Jo thought that Annette was an enabler of that kind of behavior, but she vowed that enabling was something that she would never do.

Jo went to the window and watched the little girl wave as she trotted into the store. Her red ponytails bounced with an innocence that sent chills down Jo's spine. Her vivid imagination kicked in, as she thought of the dangerous Shawn Harris lurking about in the store, ready to slice her little white throat and drink her warm blood.

"Jo?" he said again, trying to get her attention. Jo came out of her daydream.

"Oh, sorry," Jo said, as she turned around. "What did you say?"

"I said, 'Are you ready?'" Ken laughed. He spoke and accidentally spit some cheese out of his mouth obtained from a stolen bite out of Annette's sandwich. Annette laughed at him with a snort and a wink. The flirting was absolutely disgusting to Jo.

"Yeah. Let's go," Jo said and grabbed her jacket. As she walked away, she heard a few more giggles at the lab desk.

Jo was not against relationships. She was in a nasty divorce recently, and she was not in the mood. That was the attitude that greeted John Graham when she opened the door.

John was at the front door and prepared to knock, but he quickly faced the forceful Jo. She came out of her anger, as they nearly bumped into each other.

"I'm sorry," she apologized.

John was dressed in white overalls and carried a gallon of paint. He was going to paint a wall and was genuinely lost. He asked for directions, and his innocence broke Jo down.

28

"I was in another world," she said, as she gave another apology.

She gave some brief directions and smiled as they parted. He turned back, saw her watching him, and gave a smile back to her as he exited to a stairwell. It was a brief and awkward moment, but it was a breath of fresh air to Jo—and he smelled good too. She breathed in gulps of leftover cologne, as Ken tapped her on her shoulder.

"You finished, Juliet?" Ken said, as Jo pinched her lip. He walked past her, sucking the remaining cheese off his fingers in a most annoying and loud manner.

The drive to Janine's house was short, and the pair had little to say. Ken thought about Annette, and Jo thought about the painter. They avoided much conversation about the case, as each of them evaluated their next social move. It was unrealistic of Ken to think that a married woman like Annette could love him. It was equally unrealistic that Jo could love someone that probably was not as cultured as she was. That was their assessment, at least.

The apartment they found, when they arrived, was an upgrade to the previous one, the trashy one where the "Cracker" lived. Janine and Shannon lived together for several years in the broken-down building that Johnny occupied. However, even Johnny received an upgrade.

After detectives questioned Johnny for several hours, it was obvious to everyone that he never realized what was in the refrigerator. He was, however, booked on drug possession charges. Ken felt that he would be safer in a hospital jail for a few days than out on the streets. Jo actually agreed with him.

It was determined that the body of Jason Webb was in the cool box about a week or two before Jo and Ken found him. Information from a local cashier, given to the police when the news story broke on television, confirmed this. Several boxes of plastic bags were sold to a man fitting the description of Shawn, a few weeks before Mr. Webb visited Jo.

After the doorbell rang several times, the shuffling feet arrived at the door. Janine opened the door and greeted them both, but announced that she had little time for conversation.

"Come on in," she said, as she turned away.

Jo noticed how beautiful the young woman was. The African-American girl had perfect makeup, hair, and nails. Jo looked down at her neglected nails and felt inadequate. She grabbed her fingers and then stuck both of her hands into her jeans as they entered.

Once inside, Janine directed Jo and Ken to sit down on a couch, while she excused herself to the restroom.

The living room was immaculate and extremely clean. Jo thought about her house with Casey's toys and his "plants" all over his room and hallway. It was the product of having a botanist for a son. Even though it was his hobby, all hobbies produced clutter.

Janine came back, after complaining of some back pain and holding up her breasts with her arms—as if it gave some comfort. She apologized and complained openly of frequent urination, which she blamed on a kidney stone. She seemed open with nothing to hide.

She knew about the death of Jason Webb. Ken told her over the telephone a day or two earlier.

"I'm leaving this hell hole and going to a better side of town—leaving for good!" Janine said, as she sat down slowly in a large and plush recliner. "I haven't been the same since Shannon died." She adjusted herself in the chair and moaned a few times.

"Kidney stones can be painful," Jo suddenly blurted out. Ken looked at her with a look that said, "Shut up, newbie!"

"You got that right," Janine said. "I suppose you want me to talk or something?" She directed the question to Ken.

"If you were hiding something, when we questioned you before—anything at all—it's over. There is no reason not to tell us what you know," Ken asked. "Is there?"

"Who the hell is this chick?" Janine asked Ken.

Ken looked at Jo, giving her permission to answer. Jo explained in a sentence or two that she was his "associate." Janine remembered the many detectives that had questioned her at length, but Jo was new to her. She had a weird vibe about Jo.

"You and Shannon lived with Shawn. Can you think of anything that might help us track him down?" Ken asked.

Jo began to think about Jason Webb and his odd visit. She went into a daze while the woman spoke to Ken. She recalled Jason's explanation to her. He was tracking down a serial killer. That was all that she remembered—except one thing. Jason took out a twig, out of his pocket—it was a weed of some kind, like old sagebrush. He placed it on the desk, and left in anger—because Jo refused to help him without consulting the authorities. Jo later gave the twig to her son, her little botanist.

"Lady! What the hell?" Janine shouted at the inattentive Jo. "Either wake up or get the hell out of my house."

Jo apologized, and then Ken added his as well. He did not like Jo's habit of daydreaming and spacing out on things, but he knew that various oddities were often inside gifted people.

"I am going to get married. I am going to have a new life. My boyfriend just got a job at a museum—he is a security guard, and I don't

31

care. I'd rather live with the dinosaurs in the desert than to stay in this horrible place—a place with all of these hellish memories. I am going to have a new life," Janine concluded.

"Janine?" Ken begged. He knew that she was rambling.

"I don't know where that son of a bitch is. I swear!" Janine insisted. "But as for that Jason bastard—I am glad that he is dead. Shawn killed him. I'm sure of that. Now, go arrest him and get out of my house!"

Ken showed a side that Jo had not seen before. He kept a steady glance at Janine. His persistent look demanded the truth.

Jo's phone buzzed and spread further tension in the room. Janine gave her a look, and Jo turned off her phone. She revealed her nails briefly, but then she quickly placed her hands back into her pockets. After this case is over, she thought, I am going to give my body some serious attention.

"Fine. I'll tell you," Janine said. "Truth is…I feel like total dog shit. Escaping is my only answer…either that or suicide." Janine got up, as she wrapped her arms around herself—as if in some kind of pain.

"Shannon was a beautiful girl, but she only had one little damn flaw," she said. She stood and leaned against a television set. She gazed a hole in the wall as she continued.

"Chocolate drop," Janine said. "That is what he called her, the bastard. Shawn's father was against interracial marriages. He hated that little girl. Shawn hated Pamela, the little white girl, but Shawn's father hated her mother, Shannon. She had black blood in her, although not as much as me—we were half sisters. One drop is enough for some people. Jason hated Shannon's other little girl also—the fake one."

"What girl?" Jo asked. She was glued to every word.

"That was the thing, see," Janine said. "Shannon wasn't pregnant. He just thought she was."

Ken confirmed that the statement was true. He told Jo that the autopsy proved that there was no child. Shannon and her white stepdaughter were the only victims at that time.

"And now—that "racist" is dead," Janine said. "Good riddance!"

"Excuse me? What did you say about Shawn's father?" Ken asked.

"Yeah, Jason was Shawn's daddy—illegitimate," Janine said and turned to Ken. "You are such a dumb-ass!"

6

Chapter 6

"Thanks for the ride home," Jo said, as she made polite conversation. She repeated her thanks because, surprisingly, Ken was in a daze.

All the facts were reviewed on the way to Jo's house.

Jason Webb had protected his son from the authorities. He gave him an alibi. However, it was not to save his life. It was to ensure the enormous satisfaction of killing Shawn with his own bare hands. His son violated more than women. He violated nature. He was defective, and his father had known about his oddness since Shawn's childhood. Shawn hated women—especially little girls with red hair.

As a little boy, Shawn was accidentally burned by a little girl— literally. A girl with red hair once spilled hot grease on his penis and upper legs during a school camping trip. He never forgot it. He was determined to transform that single experience into a life of pure vengeance upon every single female with red hair—especially little girls. There was no official count, but police in several states confirmed the odd deaths of little girls with reddish locks. Shannon's little stepdaughter was just one of them.

Shannon took the girl in when a boyfriend was killed at a nightclub. She thought that she was doing the girl a favor. In fact, she sentenced her to death, when she hooked up with Shawn later.

Once Jason came down with cancer, he wanted nothing more than to even the score with his son before he passed away. His son was crazy. He needed to die for that—for that, and for other reasons. Jason did not want any "chocolate drops" running around his living room. Shawn had to die. It was just that simple. Of course, Jason had to die also. Shawn saw to that little detail. Nobody betrayed Shawn and got away with it—not even his dad.

A convinced Shawn once believed his father's accusations. He attempted to force his woman to have an abortion. The real truth was tragic. There was no baby. There was only racism and prejudice and misunderstanding. There was sickness, and there was ignorance—and there was death.

"Don't go and weird me out, Jo," Ken said, as he adjusted his sweaty palms on the steering wheel. He was out of his trance, but Jo was in one of her own.

That wasn't mud on her shirt, Jo thought—but what was it?

"Earth to Jo?" Ken repeated.

Jo gave her usual apology and came back to the planet and to the conversation.

"Let's just say that we entertain the idea that I actually spoke to Mr. Webb," Jo started. "Was it from a defined future or an alternate one? Did we change…"

"Nope. I said not to do that crap on me," Ken said.

"I thought that you believed in the supernatural more than I did," Jo said. He did, but it scared him at times.

Ken changed the subject and talked instead about the local news and the weather, until they went into Jo's house. Casey was waiting for his mom. The potato chips were running out. He wanted hot dogs, but his mom wanted spaghetti. That was the first argument. The second one was more direct, and it came from Ken.

"Where is the plant, Casey?" Ken asked him. The living room gave evidence of a minor disaster. While watering his plants, Casey had spilled water on the carpet.

"It's ok, Casey," Jo told him. She assured him that there would be no punishment for any accident. Ken sighed with disapproval and rolled his eyes to the ceiling. People who are not parents seem to be so much wiser than those who are. She should get out the belt, he thought.

"It's gone, mama," Casey said. He pulled out a book to prove his statement. The little flower was gone, no longer pressed between the pages.

"What do you mean it is gone?" Ken said with some unnecessary anger. The mother did not approve of the agent's attitude at all, as Jo gave Ken yet another one of her looks.

Casey told them that the little green twig with the budding flowers on it had simply disappeared.

"You remember what you told me about it?" Jo asked.

"Yeah, it's a California plant," Casey said. "Eriogonum…"

Ken interrupted him, "I've had enough of this, Jo. We don't have time to talk about plants that appeared and disappeared anyway. There is a killer out there. Somewhere in California. Yeah, we already knew that!"

Ken was thinking, "Like mother—like son." Either Jo imagined the plant, or they both had a touch of the gift. Who knew for sure, he thought.

"It was the California Buckwheat plant," Casey said in a quickly spouted sentence, and he ran away to his bedroom with a slight whimper.

Ken realized his mistake—his mouth. His apology would not be believed, so he remained silent. He started to follow Casey to apologize, but his phone rang. It was Annette.

While a gullible Ken listened to a rant and an excuse, Jo went into another trance, sat down on her couch, and stared at a soiled carpet.

Her name meant beauty and strength. But what does that mean?

How does that fit into everything?

Ken ended his call and woke up Jo.

"Annette ain't coming in tomorrow," he said. "Something about having to meet her Spanish teacher." That completely brought Jo out of her musings.

"What did you say?" Jo asked and smiled. It was all beginning to fit.

"I said.."

"Spanish teacher," Jo finished. "Call up your people. I am going to be brave and get on an airplane!" Flying was one of her major phobias that even the Air Force did not cure. She trotted to her bedroom, as she turned to him and gave him the news—just before closing her bedroom door.

"I know where Shawn is! And you can thank that little girl with the red hair!"

Ken's jaw dropped.

Did I miss something, he thought.

7

The Corvette car door slammed with a mean attitude. Shawn reflected on the last few days and what he had done. Shawn told his girlfriend that his wandering days were officially over. He called his "other" girlfriend. He ended it with only a few words.

"It's over, bitch!" he told her. That was just a few days before the new job and his new scheduled beginning. Shawn was going to sell Jason's car, and then he was going to get married. He needed, however, a new identity.

He saw a news story on television and formulated a perfect plan. He contacted his main girl.

"I got a job, baby," he told her. "Come on out. I'm ready for you. I can almost taste you."

Perhaps it was Shawn's way of avoiding little girls with red hair. His new bride was not a white woman. Maybe it was Shawn's apology—to the dozens of white girls and women he had murdered. Of course, there were a few non-white women, but they had it coming. They were going to turn him in. They were nothing but trash. They had to die. All trash has to be taken and burned, and sometimes, he literally and physically did that. Evidence was evil. It had to be destroyed.

Shawn once burned a woman's finger just to smell it. He was a curious soul. He watched in fascination as the flesh melted away. The smell of burnt leather and copper permeated his nostrils and filled him with ecstasy.

Shawn wondered if black flesh was the same. Would it have the same smell, he thought. Maybe he could burn a finger on his bride, once he was married. She wouldn't mind. She understood him. She felt sorry for him. She would let him.

41

Chapter 7

After Shawn stepped out of the silver car, he started to play with a withdrawn lighter. He smiled as he imagined the whole scenario. It had been a while since he had smelled burning skin.

Shawn's luck in California began when he saw a video that showed job applicants at a local museum. He saw his double. He saw another Shawn. We all have them, and Shawn had his.

There have been stories throughout time about such occurrences. Maybe, the devil smiled upon Shawn and gave him such gracious pity.

His name was Bryan. He was engaged to a girl in Arizona, but Shawn broke it off for him. *She* was the "bitch" that he had called. He assumed his role completely. He found her number and address in Bryan's wallet. Perhaps, later, Shawn thought, he would drive to Arizona and visit the girl in the desert town. Maybe he would burn *her* flesh and see what *she* smelled like. He loved to see white women tortured—especially the white women that had it coming to them. Bryan's future wife was beautiful. He saw a photo of her on Brian's nightstand, on the night that he killed him. She only had one major flaw. She had red hair.

Shawn loved the color of red, just not on a woman. However, his Arizona plans were not as important as his first day on the job. He was optimistic. His new life was beginning to form.

He adjusted his black tie. The clip was a little tight. He was not used to this type of uniform. The only other uniforms that he had worn were white and inside of a hospital. At first, his daddy tried to help him, but he was beyond any help. He belonged to evil. Evil gave him his heart and soul.

Shawn did not consider himself evil. Everyone said that he had issues, but they were wrong. They were the evil ones, not him! This was his chance to get it right. This was a different direction.

The guard at the gate greeted him, just near the shack.

"You must be Bryan!" the guard with the glasses said. "I made your badge last week."

For a moment, the words scared him and his brow twitched—and so did his blue eyes. They rotated back for just a second, and then he regained his composure. The guard opened the door for him and handed him his badge.

The guard approved him. He passed the test. He made it. He was inside.

He entered the small guard shack, and another employee greeted him. It was his trainer. It was Bailey.

Bailey possessed many good qualities. Bailey had good eyesight and vision. No one else had Bailey's experience at the museum. There was only one slight problem, perhaps two. Bailey was a woman, and, more importantly, Bailey had short, and very curly, red hair.

Her skin was tight against a uniform that barely fit her white skin. She had a weight problem, but everyone loved Bailey—everyone, except Bryan.

Bailey told Bryan to sit down and start reading a book on security protocol. The "thing" had given him an order. The command came from a girl that he grew to despise in only a matter of seconds.

The phone buzzed with such a jolt that it vibrated the desk. It brought Bryan out of his thoughts for a moment. He was just beginning to imagine what Bailey's burning skin would smell like.

"How can I help you?"—Bailey first gave an official line and then moved to a more cordial language.

Chapter 7

"It's for you, Bryan," Bailey said and handed him the phone. She added some caution.

"Don't make this a habit, Bryan," she told him. "We don't allow personal calls."

Bailey winked at him and stepped outside of the shack to smoke a cigarette. That was against policy also, but people liked Bailey. Eventually, however, everyone gets caught, and everyone pays their dues.

Bailey gave Bryan about ten minutes, and then she proceeded to enter the guard shack. However, she quickly found out that the new employee, Bryan, snapped, just after speaking to his future wife. Her arrival was earlier than planned. She wanted to talk to him. She had something important to say to him.

Bryan did not believe it. She had a "tone." She said that she loved him. They are all alike, he thought. Black or white—it made no difference at all. He knew what he had to do. She talked like the people in the hospital. It was a special sympathetic voice, not genuine—it was condescending.

Bailey never knew that she had smoked her last cigarette. Life was very short on that afternoon.

She came in and faced an attack the moment that the door closed. Bryan had found his screwdriver. It was his favorite. He had brought it in, just in case. He almost forgot that he had it, until it rattled against the table as he leaned over and talked with his future wife.

The tool did not work. It was not deep enough. Bryan hated complications, so he improvised. He took the phone cord and quickly wrapped it around Bailey's neck and forced her down, and then he began to softly curse at her. He knelt down at her side on the floor. He whispered in her ears and randomly plucked out strands of her hair, even after she gave her final struggle. "No one burns me," Shawn told her. He licked her ears and then stood up beside her dead body.

He kicked her in her side with his steel toe, and he was going to burn her finger. The suspense was killing him, but he had more important things to do. He had to meet his girlfriend.

Janine was waiting for him.

8

They agreed to meet in a garden, but there were many gardens—and many distractions. It took a few minutes to find the right place. To complicate matters, he walked in his security uniform without even thinking about the delays that it caused. People who wanted to know where the restrooms were, and other questions of absolute nonsense to him, interrupted him along the way.

When he finally saw her, he wiped his sweat off with his white sleeve. His face was overheated because of the unreasonable uniform that he was forced to wear on a warm day. However, he was also nervous about the words that Janine might say.

He took her to a bench, away from the general crowd, and near a closed lunch booth.

"I wanted to see you—honey," she said, after some hesitation. Her legs trembled slightly against the metal bench.

There was the tone again, he thought.

"I loved you more than Shannon, you know," he confessed. "But she had to go, baby. She was going to talk. I had to…"

"I know," Janine grabbed his hand and clenched it tightly. "I know, baby. But Shannon was only part black. I am the real thing, sugar. Come here." She pulled his head to her shoulders and pampered her baby.

"I wanted to help you so badly, honey," she said. "I truly did, baby. But I don't think that I am going to be enough for you."

Shawn felt something uncomfortable against his ear as he lay on her shoulder. He jerked back quickly and ripped her blouse open. He saw the wire on her shoulder. A brief mistake blew her cover.

Shawn got up and looked around, but he saw no one. He pulled out his screwdriver, prepared to drive it into his girlfriend's skull. Janine bent over, placed her head between her knees, and screamed, "Help me!"

Just before Shawn jammed his tool into her head, help arrived. They hid behind a rock. It was Ken and several police officers.

"Shawn!" Ken screamed. It stopped Shawn for only a moment, but he reached his arm back for a quick stab.

Ken fired and fired once more. Shawn fell back and onto the cement behind the bench. Crowds of onlookers immediately started to either scream or gather in the general vicinity. Ken ran up to Janine.

"Are you ok?" he asked her. Ken may have been a goofball to Jo, but fortunately he was one of the best shooters on his team of secret agents. Shawn was dead.

"Yeah, I think so," Janine said to Ken. She grabbed her side in pain.

Jo came running up, soon after, and she knelt before the shaken Janine. She hugged her and they both cried. Jo thanked her for trusting her and playing along with the set up.

Janine broke the tension that was between them earlier, "You need a nail job, darling." With laughter and another embrace, Jo expressed her agreement.

"And you need a hospital," Jo said. As she said it, Janine felt another pain.

"How did you know?" Janine asked her.

"Women just know," Jo told her. Then it was Jo that gave Ken the next directive, but with a gentle smile.

"Ken," she said to him. "Can you call an ambulance, please?"

"Sure," Ken said. "Probably a good idea...check her

out…trauma and all."

"She's pregnant, Ken," Jo said to the surprised agent.

9

C asey was glad to have his mother home. She even surrendered and made him hot dogs. She needed something quick. She had a date to go on. Her "man" was coming over.

The doorbell rang and Casey was sent to his room to watch his favorite documentary—it was something about plants. That was all that his mom knew.

Jo rushed to the door and welcomed the new and casually dressed style of Agent Jackson. Ken posed in various positions to impress her.

"What do you think of the new look?" he asked her.

Jo smiled brightly and reviewed his attire.

"I think you look very hot in jeans!" she told him.

"Really?" Ken said and blushed.

Jo told him to wait in the living room because she was finishing a few snacks for Casey. Casey would be hungry later, and Jo tried to be prepared. She fixed a tray of healthy veggies with dip, but she hid the potato chips. At least he will have to burn off calories while he searches for them, she thought.

"The kid is skinny," Ken said. "Let him eat what he wants. But, of course, you are the mom."

"Wise words," Jo said, as she loaded the dishwasher.

"Hey, I have waited long enough," Ken said. "I have been in California, finishing all the business out there— just dying to know. So…cough it up."

"She urinated a lot," Jo began. "She had pain in her chest and sides. It was only a hunch."

"Yeah," Ken said, as he came into the cramped but homey

kitchen. "And the museum?"

"It was what you said," Jo told him. "The little girl and her Spanish class. The girl who first came to see me was Brea. Well, I knew that the origin of the name meant strength. But I was thinking in the wrong language. Brea, in Spanish, is tar. And it was something else. Janine said that she would prefer to live in the desert with the dinosaurs. I just put them together. There was a tar pit and museum in California."

"And the weed was from California?" Ken asked.

"Who knows," she said. "Casey told me that it could have been from either California or from Arizona. Maybe it was from a future that was going to happen but never did. There were enough clues for a blind man to solve this one. Besides, Jason had mud and tar on him, on his jacket—and so did the little girl, on her feet and clothes."

"So you do believe in this?" he asked her.

"Yes," Jo said, as she walked to the coat rack, near the front door. She yelled back to Casey, and told him to behave himself.

"Mr. Jackson," she said, as she stepped close to a standing Ken. "I believe that you have yourself an official employee now."

"What about the girl?" he asked her. "Who was she? Shannon wasn't pregnant."

"No," admitted Jo. "But Janine was."

"You mean?" he started.

"That's right," Jo told him. "Her daughter is going to be named Brea. I got a phone call from her an hour ago. She is staying with a cousin and is going to have that new life—just like she promised."

"Are you ready?" Ken asked her, as he moved closer to her and looked into her sparkling eyes. He was beginning to admire this consultant, even more than Annette, or any other person he had ever worked with. Jo was different. Jo was special. Jo had possibilities. It was in her smile and in her frown. It was in her tenderness and her stable firmness.

The doorbell rang, and Jo opened the door. It was John.

"Am I late," John asked. He had cleaned up. Mr. Graham was wearing a black sports jacket and dress slacks. His polished shoes were a bonus—that, and the delicious smell of his manly cologne.

Jo looked back at Ken.

"You guys have fun!" she said and smiled back at him. The night belonged to Jo and her man.

"We will," Ken said, with some hidden disappointment. He had agreed to bond with Casey, but he had hoped that Jo would change her mind about going out. She didn't.

Jo closed the door behind her and John popped his question.

"What movie are we watching?" he asked her, as he escorted her to his compact car.

"Anything but a creepy movie," Jo told him.

We hoped that you enjoyed this short story. Please visit our website at Http://RaeTAlexander.com and feel free to leave a review at Http://www.Amazon.com.

www.ingramcontent.com/pod-product-compliance
Lightning Source LLC
Chambersburg PA
CBHW071215130626
46555CB00004B/1714